The Wisdom of Chinese Words

Reading Textbook 閱讀課本

2

Min Guo
郭敏

香港字藝出版社
Hong Kong Word Art Press

The Wisdom of Chinese Words 2 (Reading Textbook)   A Series of Textbooks of Chinese U See

Author:	Min Guo
Illustrator:	Min Guo
Editors:	Jin-li Li, Franklin Koo
Publisher:	Hong Kong Word Art Press
Address:	Unit 503, 5/F, Tower 2, Lippo Center, 89 Queensway Road, Admiralty, HK
Website:	www.wordart.com.hk/www.chineseusee.com
Edition:	First edition published in 2016, Hong Kong
Size:	215 mm × 270 mm
ISBN:	978-988-14915-4-1

漢字的智慧 2（閱讀課本）   象形卡通系列教科書

作　者：	郭　敏
繪　畫：	郭　敏
編　輯：	李金麗，顧為傑
出　版：	香港字藝出版社
地　址：	香港金鐘金鐘道 89 號力寶中心第 2 座 5 樓 503 室
網　頁：	www.wordart.com.hk/www.chineseusee.com
版　次：	2016 年香港第一次印刷
規　格：	215 mm × 270 mm
國際書號：	978-988-14915-4-1

Table of Contents
目錄

Radicals

部首

Radical 部首	Name of Radical 部首名稱	Name of Radical 部首名稱
人	人部	One Person Radical
女	女部	Female Radical
宀	宀部	Roof Top
子	子部	Child Radical
戶	戶部	Household Radical
彳	彳部	Two Person Radical
田	田部	Field Radical
土	土部	Land Radical
馬	馬部	Horse Radical
羊	羊部	Sheep Top
父	父部	Father Top
門	門部	Door Radical

Radical 部首	Name of Radical 部首名稱	Name of Radical 部首名稱
力	力部	Labour Radical
耂	老部	Senior Top
八	八部	Eight Top
走	走部	Walking Radical
四	四部	Four Top
足	足部	Foot Radical
竹	竹部	Bamboo Top
辶	辶部	Transporting Radical
小	小部	Small Top
夕	夕部	Sunset Radical
魚	魚部	Fish Radical

課文 Text

The ancient word for human. 古漢字「人」。

rén

人

human/
man

hěn jiǔ yǐ qián　　rén lèi jiù chū xiàn le
很 久 以 前 ， 人 類 就 出 現 了 。

dòng

洞

cave

tóng

同

together/
with

rén men gòng tóng zhù zài shān dòng li
人 們 共 同 住 在 山 洞 裏 。

A long time ago, human beings first appeared. People lived together in caves.

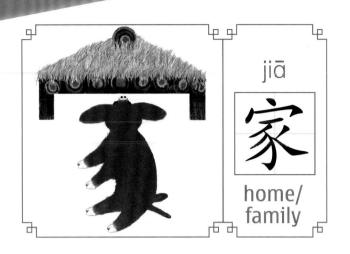

jiā

家

home/
family

tún

豕

pig/pork

dāng zhū ròu chéng wéi zhōng guó rén de zhǔ yào ròu shí shí
當豬肉成為中國人的主要肉食時，

tā men jiù dìng jū xià lai　　yǒu le gù dìng de jiā
他們就定居下來，有了固定的家。

kàn

看

see/
watch

yí gè měi lì de nǚ rén guì zài hé biān xǐ shù
一個美麗的女人跪在河邊洗漱。

yí gè nán rén kàn jiàn le tā
一個男人看見了她。

When pork became the most popular meat in China, Chinese people settled down and had a permanent home. A beautiful woman was kneeling down by a creek, washing herself. A man saw her.

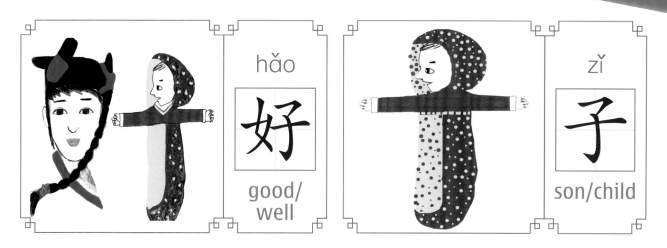

hǎo

好

good/
well

zǐ

子

son/child

tā xiǎng yǒu le nǚ rén jiù yǒu hái zi　nà gāi duō hǎo
他想有了女人就有孩子，那該多好！

tā xīn shēng àn liàn　huà le zhè ge nǚ rén de xíng xiàng
他心生暗戀，畫了這個女人的形象。

Oracle Bone Script for woman.
甲骨文1「女」。

nǚ

女

female/
woman

hòu lái　tā chéng le jiǎ gǔ wén de　nǚ　zì　rán ér
後來，它成了甲骨文的「女」字。然而

xiàn dài de　nǚ　zì què hé tā wán quán bù tóng
現代的「女」字卻和它完全不同。

He thought it would be very good to have a woman, who would give him children. He drew a picture of this woman. Later, it became the word for "woman" in Oracle Bone Script. But the modern Chinese word for "female/woman" is quite different.

3

1. The pictographs carved on turtle shells and animals' bones in ancient times. 古代刻在甲骨和獸骨上的象形文字。

Radical 14　偏旁部首（14）

Shape Radical
形旁

1)
人 — One Person Radical
會 huì — can
你 nǐ — you

2)
女 — Female Radical
好 hǎo — good
婦 fù — woman

3)
宀 — Roof Top
家 jiā — home
安 ān — safe

4)
子 — Child Radical
孫 sūn — grandson
學 xué — learn

Sound Radical
聲旁

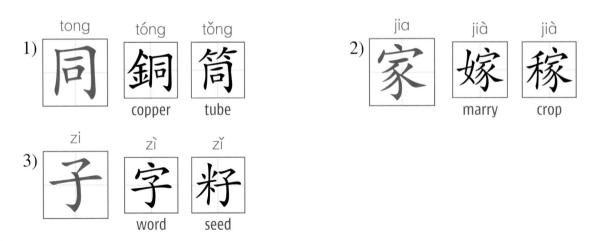

1)
同 tong
銅 tóng — copper
筒 tǒng — tube

2)
家 jia
嫁 jià — marry
稼 jià — crop

3)
子 zi
字 zì — word
籽 zǐ — seed

1. Fill in the missing words according to the Pinyin. 根據拼音組詞。

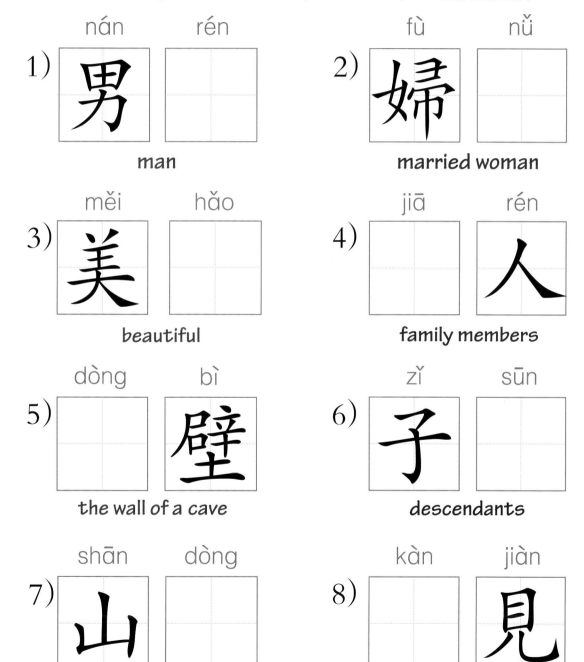

1)　nán　rén
　男　☐
man

2)　fù　nǔ
　婦　☐
married woman

3)　měi　hǎo
　美　☐
beautiful

4)　jiā　rén
　☐　人
family members

5)　dòng　bì
　☐　壁
the wall of a cave

6)　zǐ　sūn
　子　☐
descendants

7)　shān　dòng
　山　☐
mountain caves

8)　kàn　jiàn
　☐　見
seen

2. Answer the following questions. 回答下列問題。

a. Look at the ancient Chinese word " 人 ". How do you think humans came into being? 參看古代漢字「人」，你認為人類是怎樣產生的？

b. Where do you think primitive people lived? 你認為原始人住在哪裏？

c. Why do you think that the Chinese word " 好" was formed by " 女 " and " 子 "? 為甚麼漢字「好」是由「女」和「子」組成的？

d. After pork became the most popular meat in China, Chinese people settled and had a permanent home. Why do you think this happened? 當豬肉成為中國人主要的肉食時，他們就定居下來，有了固定的家，這是為甚麼？

 **Project 研究項目** **Ask three adults about how humans came into existence. 詢問三個大人「人類是怎樣出現的？」**

1._____

2._____

3._____

wǒ rèn wéi rén lèi shì shēng chu lai de
我認為人類是生出來的！
I think humans were born into this world.

課文 Text

jià
嫁
marry
(for woman)

ān
安
safe

nǚ rén jià gěi le nán rén jiù yǒu le jiā
女人嫁給了男人就有了家。

zhè ge jiā yīng gāi ràng tā jué de ān quán
這個家應該讓她覺得安全[2]。

qǔ
取
get/take

qǔ
娶
marry (for man)

nán rén qǔ de nǚ rén yīng gāi ràng tā ěr gēn qīng jìng
男人娶的女人應該讓他耳根清淨[2]。

When a woman married a man, she would have a home. In this home she should feel safe. When a man married a lady, she should make his home peaceful.

2. The ancient Chinese philosophy is shown in the word formations. 這是漢字結構中的古代哲學。

fáng

房

house

hù

户

household

jǐ hù rén jia zài yì qǐ gài fáng zi
幾戶人家在一起蓋房子，

tā men de qīn qi hé péng you yě bān le guò lai
他們的親戚和朋友也搬了過來。

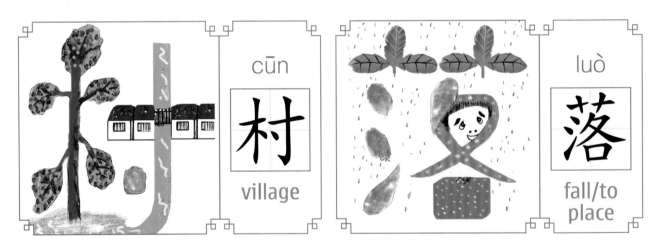

cūn

村

village

luò

落

fall/to place

hòu lái zhè ge dì fang xíng chéng le cūn luò
後來這個地方形成了村落。

nà shí mǔ xì shè huì shǒu xiān chū
那時母系社會出現了。

Several families built their houses together. Then their relatives and friends moved over. Later, this place became a village. A matriarchal society came into being at that time..

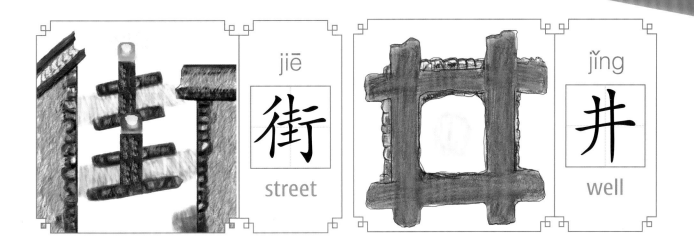

jiē
街
street

jǐng
井
well

zhōng guó rén hěn zǎo yǐ qián jiù yǒu jiē dào hé shuǐ jǐng
中國人很早以前就有街道和水井。

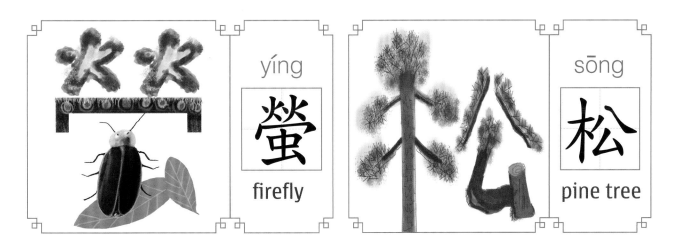

yíng
螢
firefly

sōng
松
pine tree

zhōng guó yě shì zuì zǎo shǐ yòng dēng de guó jiā zhī yī
中國也是最早使用燈的國家之一。

zuì chū de dēng shì yíng huǒ chóng hé sōng shù yóu zuò de
最初的燈是螢火蟲和松樹油做的。

Chinese people were the first in the world to have streets and water wells. China was also one of the first countries to know how to make lights. Their first lamps and candles were made from fireflies and rosin.

Radical 15   偏旁部首（15）

Shape Radical
形旁

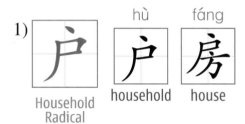

1)

	hù	fáng
户	户	房
Household Radical	household	house

2)

	xíng	jiē
彳	行	街
Two People Radical	walking	street

Sound Radical
聲旁

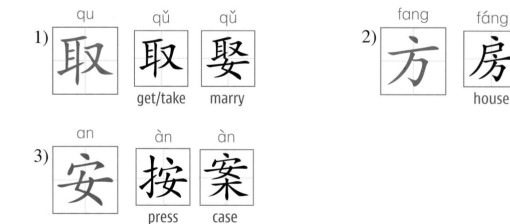

1)

qu	qǔ	qǔ
取	取	娶
	get/take	marry

2)

fang	fáng	fàng
方	房	放
	house	set free

3)

an	àn	àn
安	按	案
	press	case

1. Fill in the missing words according to the Pinyin. 根據拼音組詞。

1) ān quán
全 ☐
safe

2) jiē dào
☐ 道
street

3) fáng zi
☐ 子
house

4) jià qǔ
☐ 娶
marry

5) shuǐ jǐng
水 ☐
water well

6) yíng guāng
☐ 光
fluoresence

7) shān cūn
山 ☐
mountain village

8) chóng zi
☐ 子
insect/bug

2. Answer the following questions. 回答下列問題。

a. According to the word formation, what did an ancient Chinese boy or a girl need to remember when she or he was going to marry someone? 根據漢字結構，在古代的中國，當男孩兒和女孩兒要結婚時，他們要記住甚麼？

b. How did a village come into being? 村落是怎樣產生的？

c. What was present in a village? 村裏有甚麼？

d. What was the significance of water wells? 水井的意義是甚麼？

Project 研究項目 **How do you think cities were formed? There are three main reasons:** 城市是怎樣產生的（網上查詢或詢問大人）？ 試述三個主要原因：

1._____

2._____

3._____

wǒ rèn wéi shì yóu yú yǒu shāngdiàn
我認為是由於有商店。
I think because of the shops.

3

課文 Text

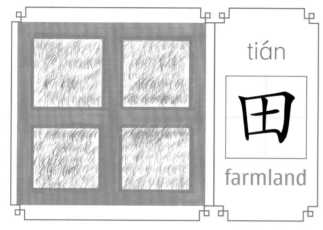

tián
田
farmland

tǔ
土
soil/land

郭家地

rén men zài cūn biān zhòng tián　mǒi jiā dōu yǒu tǔ dì
人們在村邊種田。每家都有土地。

mǎ
馬
horse

niú
牛
cattle

yǎng mǎ wèi le tuó wù　yǎng niú wéi le lí dì
養馬為了馱物，養牛為了犁地。

People planted rice near their villages. Every family owned some farmland. Horses were domesticated to carry heavy things and cattle were tamed to plough the farmlands.

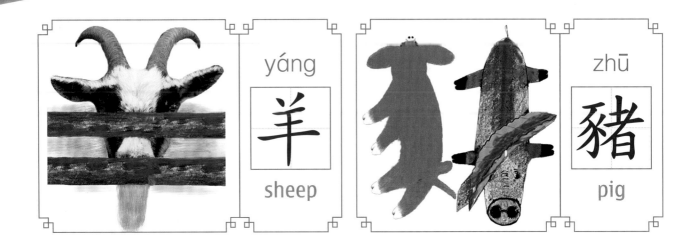

yǎng yáng wèi le chī ròu　　yǎng zhū wèi le yǎng jiā
養羊為了吃肉，養豬為了養家[3]。

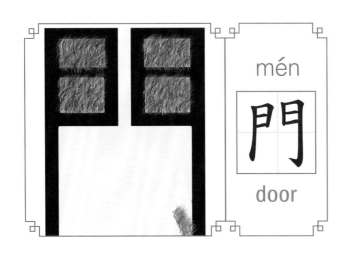

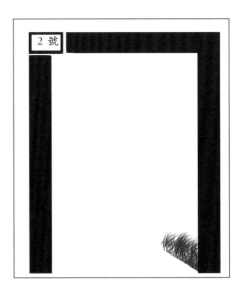

zhè shì gǔ dài de mén　　jiǎn tǐ zì de mén shì mén kuàng
這是古代的門，簡體字的門是門框。

Sheep were raised for meat. People bred pigs to support their families.
This is the ancient word for door. The simplified word for door is only a frame.

3. The Chinese word " 養 " is formed by the Sheep Top Radical and food/eat. 漢字的「養」是由「羊字頭」和「食」組成的。

chuǎng 闖 rush

mā 媽 mother

mǎ chuǎng jin le jiā mén　　mā ma jiāng mǎ lā zǒu le
馬 闖 進 了 家 門 。 媽 媽 將 馬 拉 走 了 。

bà 爸 father

yé 爺 grandfather

zhè shì bà ba de bà ba　　wǒ jiào tā yé ye
這 是 爸 爸 的 爸 爸 ， 我 叫 他 爺 爺 。

tā yǒu yī gè dà xià ba　　tā xǐ huān dǎ dǔn
他 有 一 個 大 下 巴 ， 他 喜 歡 打 盹 。

A horse rushed through the door. Mother pulled the horse away.
This is my father's father. I call him grandfather. He has a big jaw, and he likes to take a nap.

Radical 16　偏旁部首（16）

Shape Radical 形旁

1)
田	略 luè	苗 miáo
Farm Radical	strategy	seedling

2)
土	去 qù	城 chéng
Land Radical	go	city

3)
馬	馱 tuó	駒 jū
Horse Radical	carry	foal

4)
羊	美 měi	羔 gāo
Sheep Top	beauty	lamb

5)
父	爸 bà	爺 yé
Father Top	father	grandfather

6)
門	問 wèn	閃 shǎn
Door Radical	ask	sparkle

Sound Radical 聲旁

1)
馬 ma	螞 mǎ	罵 mà
	ant	curse

2)
羊 yang	洋 yáng	樣 yáng
	ocean	appearance

3)
門 men	悶 mèn	們 men
	boring	plural

1. Fill in the missing words according to the Pinyin. 根據拼音組詞。

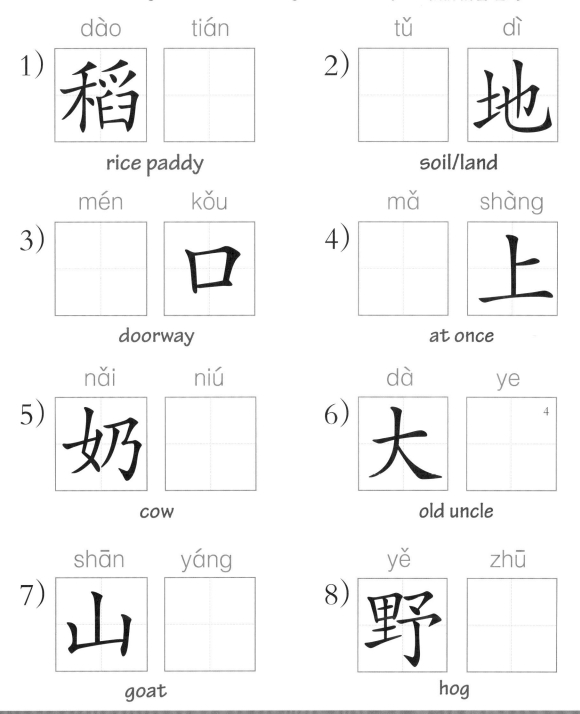

1)　dào　tián
　　稲　□
　　rice paddy

2)　tǔ　dì
　　□　地
　　soil/land

3)　mén　kǒu
　　□　口
　　doorway

4)　mǎ　shàng
　　□　上
　　at once

5)　nǎi　niú
　　奶　□
　　cow

6)　dà　ye
　　大　□ 4
　　old uncle

7)　shān　yáng
　　山　□
　　goat

8)　yě　zhū
　　野　□
　　hog

4. "大爺" is a relative and a title of respect. 「大爺」是親戚，也是尊稱。

2. Answer the following questions. 回答下列問題。

a. Why do we breed different domestic animals for? 為甚麼我們要養不同的家畜？

b. Why did breeding pigs help to provide a living for the whole family? 為甚麼養豬是為了養家？

c. What other things can cattle do for us? 牛還能為我們做甚麼？

d. Why do you think the Chinese word for 「媽」 is formed by the words 「女」 and 「馬」? 為甚麼漢字「媽」是由「女」和「馬」字組成的？

Project 研究項目　How did primitive men make a living? 原始村落的人們是怎樣生存的？

1._____

2._____

3._____

zì gěi zì zú
自給自足！
Self-sufficiency!

4

課文 Text

力
lì
labour/power

男
nán
male/man

zài zhōng guó gǔ dài nán rén shì tián li zhǔ yào de láo dòng lì
在中國古代，男人是田裏主要的勞動力。

老
lǎo
old/senior

孩
hái
children

lǎo rén zhào gù hái zi nǚ rén zuò jiā wù
老人照顧孩子。女人做家務。

In ancient China, men were the main labourers on the farm. The senior people took care of the children. The women did the housework.

奶 nǎi　grand-mother

妻 qī　wife

nǎi nai shì wǒ yé ye de qī zi
奶奶[5]是我爺爺[6]的妻子。

tā de yì zhī ěr duo bú tài hǎo shǐ le
她的一隻耳朵不太好使了！

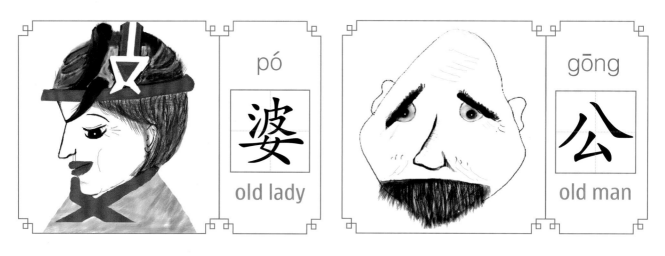

婆 pó　old lady

公 gōng　old man

wài pó ài shēng qì wài gōng de méi máo shì bā zì méi
外婆[7]愛生氣，外公[8]的眉毛是八字眉。

Grandma is my grandfather's wife. One of her ears does not work very well. Grandma (on mother's side) is always angry. My grandpa (on mother's side) has long droopy eyebrows.

5. " 奶奶 " is father's mother. 「奶奶」是爸爸的媽媽。 6. " 爺爺 " father's father. 「爺爺」是爸爸的爸爸。 7. " 外婆 " is mother's moth
「外婆」是媽媽的媽媽。 8. " 外公 " is mother's father. 「外公」是媽媽的爸爸。

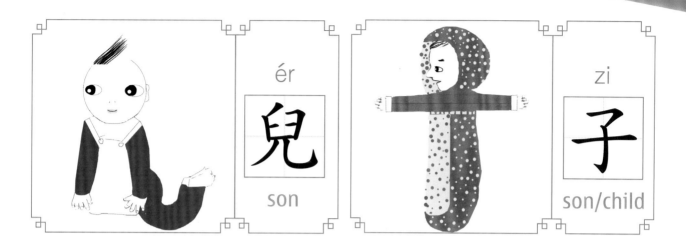

ér
兒
son

zi
子
son/child

sūn zi shì ér zi de ér zi   shì dí xì zǐ sūn
孫子是兒子的兒子，是嫡系子孫。

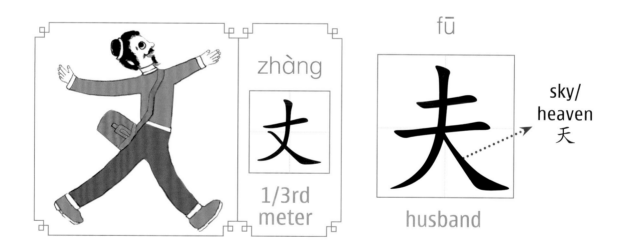

zhàng
丈
1/3rd
meter

fū
夫
sky/
heaven
天
husband

dà zhàng fu dǐng tiān lì dì
大 丈 夫 頂 天 立 地 。

qiáo   tiān dōu bèi tā dǐng pò le
瞧 ， 天 都 被 他 頂 破 [9] 了 ！

A grandson is the son's son. He is the direct desendant of his grandfather. A real man's
back is always upright. Look, the sky is pierced by him (causing great trouble).

9. " 天 " also means the emperor, who was called the son of God. This phrase means he caused serious trouble. 「天」也有皇帝的意思。
皇帝被稱為天子。這個短句的意思是「他闖大禍了！」

Radical 17　偏旁部首（17）

Shape Radical
形旁

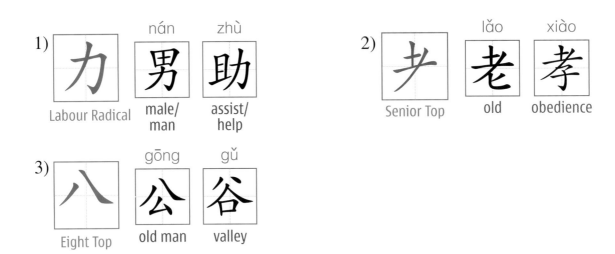

1)
力 — Labour Radical
男 nán — male/man
助 zhù — assist/help

2)
耂 — Senior Top
老 lǎo — old
孝 xiào — obedience

3)
八 — Eight Top
公 gōng — old man
谷 gǔ — valley

Sound Radical
聲旁

1)
亥 ai
該 gāi — should
孩 hái — children

2)
公 song
松 sōng — a pine tree
訟 sòng — litigate

3)
丈 zhang
杖 zhàng — cane
仗 zhàng — battle

4)
夫 fu
扶 fú — support
伕 fū — labour

 練習

1. Fill in the missing words according to the Pinyin. 根據拼音組詞。

1)
hái   zi

子

children

2)
nán   rén

人

man

3)
dà   jiā

大

everyone

4)
niú   nǎi

牛

milk

5)
wài   pó

外

grandmother

6)
wài   gōng

外

grandfather

7)
zhàng   fu

丈

husband

8)
sūn   nǚ

孫

granddaughter

2. Answer the following questions. 回答下列問題。

a. "The youngest son and the eldest grandson are the very life of an old lady? " What aspect of Chinese culture does this old saying reflect? 「小兒子，大孫子，老太太的命根子。」這句俗話反映了中國文化的哪些問題？

b. What does it mean if a person has "8:20" eyebrows in Chinese? 「那個人長着八點二十的眉毛」，這句話是甚麼意思？

c. What should a husband be in ancient China? 中國古代的丈夫應該是甚麼樣的人？

> *Project*
> 研究項目

Name three things our parents have taught us. 列出父母教會我們的三件事。

1. _____

2. _____

3. _____

wǒ bà ba jiāo huì wǒ zhuō yú

我爸爸教會我捉魚。

My daddy taught me how to catch fish.

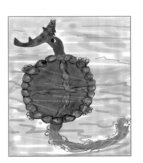

5

課文 Text

gē

哥

elder brother

zǒu

走

walk

gē ge zhèng zài tī qiú　　zhè shí xiǎo zhào cóng nà bian zǒu lai
哥哥正在踢球。這時小趙從那邊走來，

zú

足

foot

The ancient word for foot. 古漢字「足」。[10]

zú qiú tī zài tā de liǎn shang
足球踢在他的臉上。

Elder brother was playing soccer. At this time, Xiao Zhao walked over. The soccer ball was kicked onto his face.

25

10. This picture has been changed to allow students to easily understand it. 這個古字已經形象化，便於學生認識。

zhào 趙 a surname

jiū 赳 valiantly

xiǎo zhào méi you zé guài wǒ gē ge
小趙沒有責怪我哥哥，

réng jiù xióng jiū jiū de zǒu zhe
仍舊雄赳赳地走着。

tàng/tāng 趟 measure word

gǎn 趕 drive

xiǎo zhào měi tiān zài cūn li zǒu yí tàng
小趙每天在村裏走一趟，

gǎn lǎn rén xià dì gàn huó
趕懶人下地幹活。

Xiao Zhao did not blame my elder brother, and he still walked on confidently. He walked once around the village each day, driving lazy men out to do the farm work.

qǐ
起
get up

jǐ
己
self

duì bu qǐ　　qǐ lai gàn huó qu
「對不起，起來幹活去！
nǐ zì jǐ kàn kan jǐ diǎn le
你自己看看幾點了！」

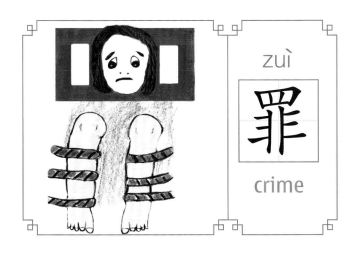

zuì
罪
crime

xiǎozhào de gōng zuò tài
小趙的工作太
dé zuì rén le
得罪人了！

Xiao Zhao's job really offended people.

lǎn duò jǐ hū jiù shì yì zhǒng zuì è
懶惰幾乎就是一種罪惡。

"Sorry. Get up, go to work. Look at the time, yourself !" Being lazy is almost a crime.

Radical 18　偏旁部首（18）

Shape Radical 形旁

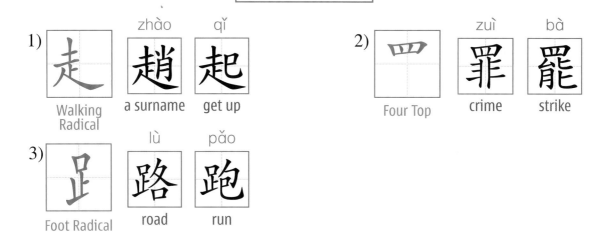

1)　走　Walking Radical　趙 zhào a surname　起 qǐ get up

2)　罒 Four Top　罪 zuì crime　罷 bà strike

3)　足 Foot Radical　路 lù road　跑 pǎo run

Sound Radical 聲旁

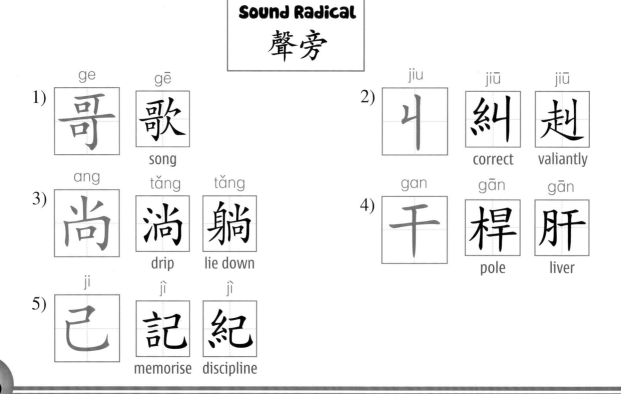

1)　哥 ge　歌 gē song

2)　丩 jiu　糾 jiū correct　赳 jiū valiantly

3)　尚 ang　淌 tǎng drip　躺 tǎng lie down

4)　干 gan　桿 gān pole　肝 gān liver

5)　己 ji　記 jì memorise　紀 jì discipline

練習

1. Fill in the missing words according to the Pinyin. 根據拼音組詞。

1)   dà   gē

大 ☐

elder brother

2)   liǎng   tàng

兩 ☐

two rounds

3)   qǐ   lai

☐ 來

get up

4)   xíng   zǒu

行 ☐

walk

5)   zú   qiú

☐ 球

soccer

6)   zì   jǐ

自 ☐

oneself

7)   gǎn   zǒu

☐ 走

drive away

8)   zuì   fàn

☐ 犯

criminal

2. Answer the following questions. 回答下列問題。

a. What is the difference between the ancient and modern words for " 足 "?
古代和現代的「足」字有甚麼不同？

b. In which country did soccer originate? 足球起源於哪裏？

c. What kind of person is Xiao Zhao? 小趙是怎麼樣的人？

d. What is regarded as the greatest virtue in China? 在中國甚麼被認為是最大的
美德？

Project
研究項目 **Find out what virtues Chinese would like to have?** 找出中國還有
哪些傳統美德？

1._____

2._____

3._____

wǒ zhī dào tā men ài chī cài
我知道他們愛吃菜。
I know they like to eat vegtables.

qiě

且

even/just

jiě jie bú dàn gàn jiā wù
姐姐不但幹家務，

ér qiě hái yào bāng mā ma zhòng cài
而且還要幫媽媽種菜。

mèi
妹
younger sister

wèi
未
not yet

mèi mei hái wèi zhǎng dà   shén me shì dōu gàn bu liǎo
妹妹還未長大，甚麼事都幹不了。

Elder sister not only did the housework, but she also helped mother to plant vegetables. Her younger sister was still very young and she couldn't do anything.

31

11. " 姊 " is formal usage, " 姐 " is also used in oral and writing. 「姊」是正式的用法。「姐」也用於口語和書寫中。

dì
弟
younger brother

dì
第
a function word

dì di xǐ huan dào lì
弟弟喜歡倒立。

bǐ sài shí tā zǒng dé dì yī míng
比賽時他總得第一名。

zhú
竹
bamboo

tā kào zhú zi dào lì
他靠竹子倒立。

tā de rèn wù shì chuán dì xiāo xi
他的任務是傳遞消息。

Younger brother enjoyed doing handstands. He was always the best at this game.
He did handstands against bamboo. His task was to pass over information.

bó 伯 elder uncle

bái 白 white

bó bo shì zhòng bái cài de　tā shuō
伯伯是種白菜的，他説：

cháng chī bái cài néng cháng mìng bǎi suì
「常吃白菜能長命百歲」。

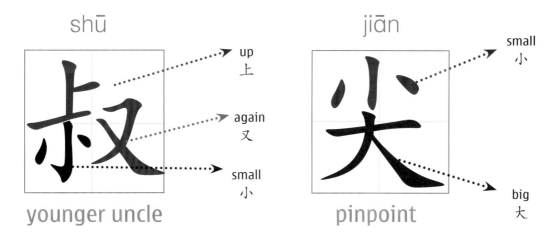

shū
叔
→ up 上
→ again 又
→ small 小
younger uncle

jiān
尖
→ small 小
→ big 大
pinpoint

shū shu bǐ bà ba xiǎo
叔叔比爸爸小。

xiǎo de zǒng shì yào bá jiān
小的總是要拔尖。

zhōng guó bú shì nǚ shì yōu xiān
中國不是女士優先。

Elder uncle planted Chinese cabbages. He said, "Eating cabbages will make people live up to one hundred years." Younger uncle is younger than my father. In China, the youngest is always considered first, unlike "ladies first" in western culture.

Radical 19　偏旁部首（19）

Shape Radical
形旁

1)

竹
Bamboo Top

dì
第
a function word

xiào
笑
laugh

2)

辶
Transporting Radical

zhè
這
this

sòng
送
send

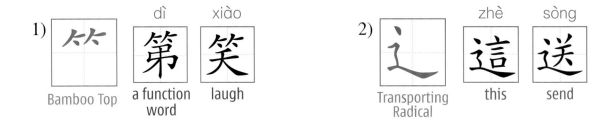

Sound Radical
聲旁

1)

di
弟

dì
第
a function word

dì
睇
look sideways

2)

bo
白

bó
伯
elder uncle

bó
泊
park

3)

shu
叔

shū
淑
fair

shū
菽
beans

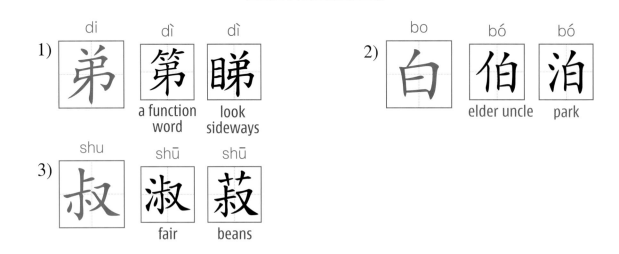

1. Fill in the missing words according to the Pinyin. 根据拼音组词。

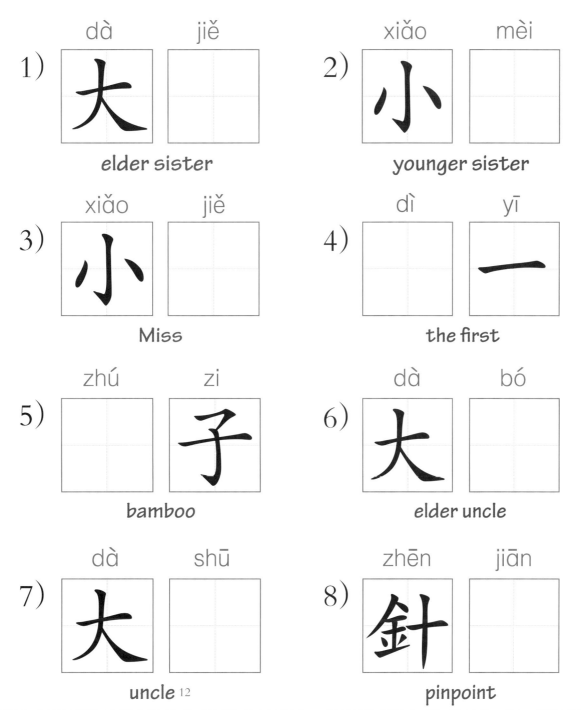

1) dà jiě
大 □
elder sister

2) xiǎo mèi
小 □
younger sister

3) xiǎo jiě
小 □
Miss

4) dì yī
□ 一
the first

5) zhú zi
□ 子
bamboo

6) dà bó
大 □
elder uncle

7) dà shū
大 □
uncle [12]

8) zhēn jiān
針 □
pinpoint

12. " 大伯 "and " 大叔 "are relatives or titles of respect. 「大伯」和「大叔」是 親戚或禮貌稱呼。

2. Answer the following questions. 回答下列問題。

a. Why does the elder sister have to do so much housework in China? 為甚麼在中國大姐要做很多的家務？

b. Why is it "The youngest first, not ladies first in China"? 為甚麼中國是「大的讓著小的」，而不是女士優先？

c. What are the different responsibilities of a man and a woman in a traditional Chinese family? 在一個傳統的中國家庭中男人和女人不同的責任是甚麼？

d. What are the responsibilities of grandparents and children in the family? 老人和孩子的家庭責任是甚麼？

Project 研究項目 What are the differences between a traditional Chinese family and a Western family? 傳統中國的家庭和西方的家庭有甚麼不同之處？

_____

_____

_____

_____

_____

7

課文 Text

yí
姨
aunt
(mother's sisters)

yí
夷
foreign (ancient)

yí lái zì dōng yí　　shuō míng mǔ qīn de niáng jiā
姨來自東夷，說明母親的娘家

zài yáo yuǎn de wài zú
在遙遠的外族。

niáng
娘
girl/mum

liáng
良
kind

shàn liáng de　gū niang cái néng zuò　yì míng hǎo mǔ qīn
善良的姑娘才能做一名好母親[13]。

" 姨 (aunt on mother's side)" came from a foreign tribe, meaning mother's family lived in a far away place. A kind-hearted girl could make a good mother.

37

13. " 母親 "are formal words for mother. 「母親」是媽媽的正式用語。 "父親" formal words for father. 「父親」是爸爸的正式用語。

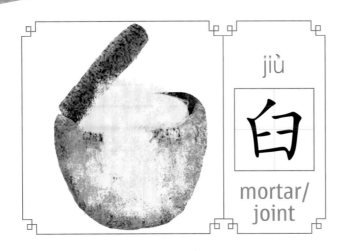

jiù
白
mortar/
joint

jiù
舅
uncle (mother's
brothers)

gǔ dài mò miàn de guàn jiào　jiù　　xiàn zài duō zhǐ guān jié
古代磨面的罐叫「白」，現在多指關節。

jiù jiu shì mā ma de xiōng di
舅舅是媽媽的兄弟。

gū
姑
aunt
(father's sisters)

gǔ
古
ancient

gū gu shì bà ba de jiě mèi
姑姑是爸爸的姊妹。

A mortar (白) is a container for grinding grains in ancient times. Now it means a joint. Uncle (舅舅) is a mother's brother. Aunt (姑姑) is a father's sister.

sǒu

sǎo

嫂
sister-in-law

叟
a Sound Radical

sǎo zi shì wài guó rén
嫂子是外國人。

shěn

shěn

嬸
aunt-in-law

審
examine

shěn zi yě shì wài guó rén
嬸子也是外國人。

tā fù zé shěn chá zhàng mù
她負責審查賬目。

Sister-in-law is a foreigner. Aunt-in-law is also a foreigner. She is responsible for checking the accounts.

Radical 20　偏旁部首（20）

Sound Radical
聲旁

1)
liang	láng	làng
良	狼	浪
	wolf	wave

2)
gu	gù	gū
古	故	姑
	former/story	aunt

3)
sou	sōu	sōu
叟	搜	艘
	search	a measure word

4)
shen	shén	shēn
審	嬸	瀋
	aunt-in-law	a place name

wǒ shì lǎo wài
我是老外，
lái zì hǎi wài
來自海外！

1. Write out the words according to the cartoons. 看圖寫字。

2. Answer the following questions. 回答下列問題。

a. Why did mother's family live so far away? 為甚麼媽媽的娘家在遠方？

b. What do you call father's brothers and sisters?　你怎樣稱呼爸爸的兄弟姐妹？

c. What do you call mother's brothers and sisters?　你怎樣稱呼媽媽的兄弟姐妹？

**Project
研究項目**　**Choose one of the following topics as your project. Then make use of the Internet to search for answers.** 選擇其中一個題目做研究項目，利用網絡資源搜索答案。

a. What is " 紅娘 "? Why is she very important in Chinese culture? 甚麼是「紅娘」？為甚麼她在中國文化中很重要？

_____

_____

_____

b. How does a country come into being?　一個國家是怎樣產生的？

_____

_____

_____

8

課文 Text

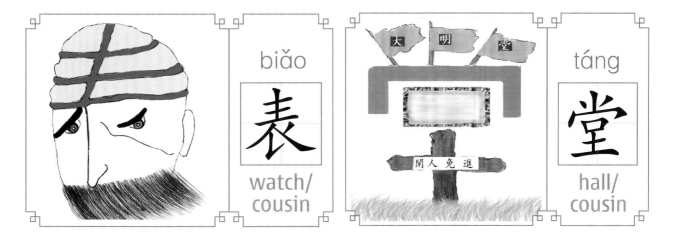

biǎo
表
watch/cousin

táng
堂
hall/cousin

閒人免進

大 明 堂

tā de biǎo gē shì wǒ de táng xiōng
他 的 表 哥 是 我 的 堂 兄[14]。

nǐ
你
you

nín
您
you (respect)

yì bān rén chēng nǐ biǎo shì zūn zhòng shí chēng nín
一 般 人 稱「你」，表 示 尊 重 時 稱「您」。

His cousin on his mother's side is my cousin on my father's side. "你" is used for general people. "您" is a title of respect.

14. "表兄弟" and "表姐妹" are cousins on mother's side. 「表兄弟」和「表姐妹」是媽媽的親戚。 "堂兄弟" and "堂姐妹" are cousins on father's side. 「堂兄弟」和「堂姐妹」是爸爸的親戚。

xìng
姓
surname

shēng
生
bear/produce

zuì chū rén men suí mǔ qīn de xìng
最初人們隨母親的姓。

hòu lái cái suí fù qīn de xìng
後來才隨父親的姓。

xī
夕
sunset

míng
名
name

xī yáng luò shān hòu　　bú yào dà shēng jiào
夕陽落山後，不要大聲叫

bié rén de míng zi
別人的名字。

In the beginning, people took their mothers' surnames. Later they took their fathers' names as their surnames. After sunset, don't yell out other people's names.

jù shuō zài wǎn shang guǐ jiào rén míng
據說在晚上鬼叫人名，

rú guǒ nǐ dā ying　　tā jiù jiāng nǐ dài zǒu
如果你答應，它就將你帶走。

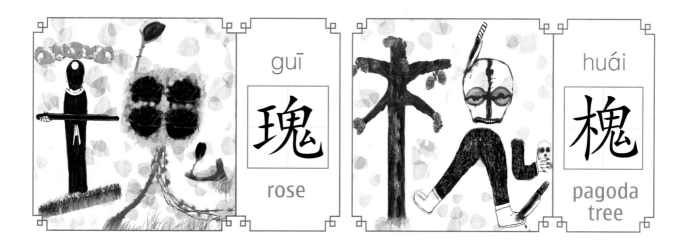

chuán shuō nǚ guǐ shì huái shù xià de méi guī biàn chéng de
傳說女鬼是槐樹下的玫瑰變成的。

It was said that the ghost would call people's names at night. If you answered, it would take you away. The female ghosts would drift out from a rose under the pagoda tree in the tale.

45

Radical 21　偏旁部首（21）

Shape Radical　形旁

1)

 小　Small Top

堂 táng　hall/cousin

黨 dǎng　party (politics)

2)

 夕　Sunset Radical

夢 mèng　dream

名 míng　name

Sound Radical　聲旁

1)

也 ta/chi

他 tā　he

她 tā　she

馳 chí　gallop

池 chí　pool

2)

生 xing/sheng

姓 xìng　surname

性 xìng　gender

星 xīng　star

牲 shēng　animal

3)

我 e

餓 è　hungry

鵝 é　goose

1. Write out the words according to the cartoons. 看圖寫字。

2. Answer the following questions. 回答下列問題。

a. Why did people use their mother's surname at first? 為甚麼最初人們隨母姓？

b. Why shouldn't we yell out other's names after sunset? 為甚麼夕陽落山以後，我們不能大聲叫別人的名字？

c. Why did the ghost yell people's names at night? 為甚麼鬼會在夜裏叫人名？

Project 研究項目 **Choose one of the following topics as your project. 選擇其中一個題目做研究項目。**

1. Tell a ghost story. 講一個鬼的故事。

_____

_____

_____

2. How do you explain the word " 罪 " according to the cartoon? 參照卡通你怎樣解釋「罪」這個字？

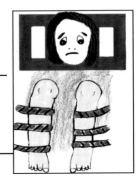

_____

_____

9

課文 Text

nián
年
year

jié
節
festival

zhōng guó xīn nián shì zhōng guó rén zuì zhòng yào de jié rì

中國新年是中國人最重要的節日。

chūn
春
spring

tiān
天
day/the sky

zhōng guó xīn nián shì chūn tiān de dì yī tiān

中國新年是春天的第一天，

suǒ yǐ jiào chūn jié

所以叫春節。

Chinese New Year is the major festival of the year. It is also the first day of the spring, so it is also called the Spring Festival.

kāi
開
open

yè
夜
night

chūn jié de qián yì tiān　dāng xī yáng luò shān shí

春節的前一天，當夕陽落山時，

chú xī yè kāi shǐ le　měi ge rén dōu zhǎng le yí suì

除夕夜開始了，每個人都長了一歲。

kè
客
guest

gè
各
individual

měi jiā měi hù dōu yǒu hěn duō kè rén

每家每戶都有很多客人，

gè zì dōu dài zhe lǐ wù

各自都帶着禮物。

The day before Chinese New Year is Chinese New Year's Eve. When the sun sets down, everyone will become one year older. Every household will have many guests, all of them bringing various gifts.

xiào
笑
laugh

jiào
叫
bark/
cry/call

lǎo rén men xiào　　hái zi men nào　　gǒu yě jiào
老人們笑，孩子們鬧，狗也叫，
dà jiā dōu hěn gāo xìng
大家都很高興。

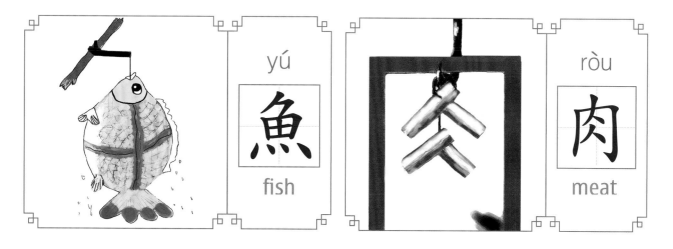

yú
魚
fish

ròu
肉
meat

jiā jiā de cān zhuō shang dōu bǎi fàng zhe
家家的餐桌上都擺放着
dà yú hé dà ròu
大魚和大肉。

*Old people are laughing, little children are joyful, even the dogs are barking around them.
Everyone is happy. Every family's dinner table is filled with large plates of fish and meat.*

Radical 22　偏旁部首（22）

Shape Radical
形旁

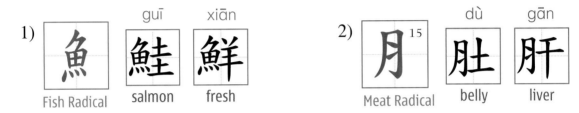

1)

魚	鮭 guī	鮮 xiān
Fish Radical	salmon	fresh

2)

月 15	肚 dù	肝 gān
Meat Radical	belly	liver

Sound Radical
聲旁

1)

各 ge	格 gé	閣 gé
	square	cabinet

2)

魚 yu	漁 yú
	fishing

Special Tops
特殊字頭

Pay attention to the writing of the words above. The tops are different. The titles of their radicals are the lower parts of the words. 註意特殊字頭的書寫，它們是不一樣的。這些字的偏旁名稱是字的下半部分。

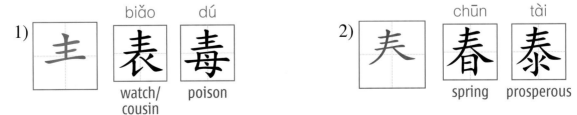

1)

主	表 biǎo	毒 dú
	watch/cousin	poison

2)

夫	春 chūn	泰 tài
	spring	prosperous

15. The two horizontal lines of Meat Radical are not straight, e.g. " 肝 ". The two horizontal lines of Moon Radical are straight, e.g. " 骨 ".
月肉旁的兩條橫線不是直的，如：「肝」。月字旁的兩條橫線是直的，如：「勝」字（修正第一冊的錯誤）。

1. Write out the words according to the cartoons. 看圖寫字。

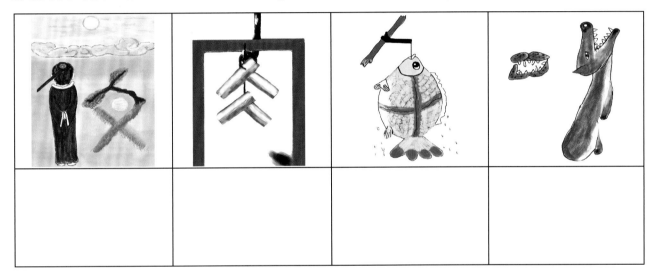

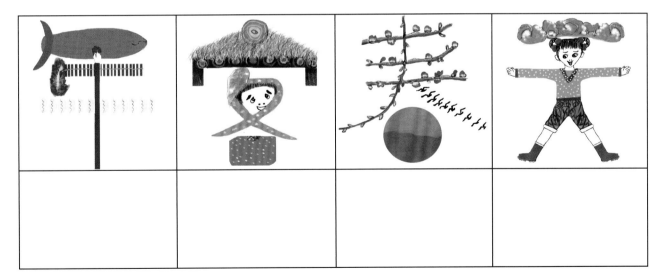

2. Answer the following questions. 回答下列問題。

a. What do Chinese people eat during the Spring Festival? 中國人春節吃甚麼？

b. What kind of guests will they entertain during the Spring Festival? 春節的時候都有甚麼客人？

c. Could you guess what kinds of gifts the guests will bring? 你能猜一猜客人會帶甚麼樣的禮物？

3. Reading comprehension. 閱讀理解。

　　我叫趙小春，今年八歲。我是元旦那天出生的。我家有爸爸、媽媽、姐姐、哥哥、弟弟、妹妹，還有爺爺和奶奶。我家一共有九口人。我的外婆住在很遠的地方。過年的時候，我們去他們家作客，給他們帶去很多禮物。我有六個舅舅和三個小姨。大家都很高興，我們吃了許多美食，每天都有魚和肉。大人還給我們壓歲錢。

Answer the following questions: 回答下列問題：

1) 趙小春出生在哪天？

_____

2) 他的爺爺奶奶住在哪裏？

_____

3) 誰是他家第一個孩子？

_____

4) 他外婆家有幾口人？

_____

5) 寫三個關於你家的句子。

_____

_____

_____

Project
研究項目

Write out the words according to the cartoons. Each word on the following couplets for Spring Festival has a meaning and a cultural content. What do you think it is? 參照卡通寫出春聯上的漢字。每個漢字都有一個意思和文化內涵。你認為是甚麼？

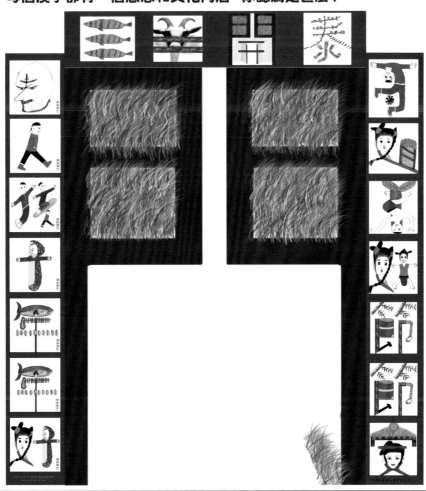

Exercise 1 P.5　練習 1　第 5 頁

1. 1）人　　2）女　　3）好　　4）家　　5）洞　　6）孫　　7）山　　8）婦

2. a. From the image of the ancient word " 人 ", we can see that humans could not stand up straight at that time, so probably humans evolved from apes. 從古代漢字「人」的形象來看，那時候的人類還不能直立行走，所以很可能人類是猴子進化而來的。

   b. Primitive people might live in trees, in caves, under cliffs, in huts and other places. 原始人也許住在樹上、山洞裏、石崖或窩棚裏等。

   c. The Chinese word " 好 (good)" is formed by " 女 (female)" and " 子 (son)" , which means it is good to have a family. Some people also think that it is good to have a daugter and a son because " 女 " also means a daughter and " 子 " means a son. 漢字「好」是「女」和「子」構成的，意思是有家人真好。「女」也可以說是女兒，「子」是兒子，所以有些人認為「有兒有女才是好。」

   d. Sheep and cattle moved from one grassland to another in different seasons, unlike pigs or hogs which always stay in the same place. So when pork became the popular meat in ancient times, the Chinese people settled down in one place. Then they made a permanent home. 豬不像牛和羊隨著季節的變化，要從一片草原移到另一片草原。野豬會在一個固定的地方生存，因此古代當豬肉成為中國人的主要肉食的時候，他們就在一個地方住了下來，有了固定的家。

Project 研究項目

1. Religious people believe that God created humans. 宗教人士認為人類是由上帝創造的。
2. Many scientists believe that humans evolved from apes. 科學家認為人類是由猿猴演化的。
3. There are even some people who believe that humans came from other planets in outer space. 有些人認為人類來自於外星球。

Exercise 2 P.11　練習 2　第 11 頁

1. 1）安　　2）街　　3）房　　4）嫁　　5）井　　6）燈　　7）村　　8）蟲

2. a. An ancient Chinese girl would consider whether her new home was safe for her. An ancient Chinese boy might wonder whether the girl he was going to marry could give him a peaceful life. 古代的中國姑娘會考慮新家對她是否安全。古代的中國男子也許會考慮他要娶的女人是否會使他安靜地生活。

   b. Relatives and friends built their homes together, then a village came into being. 親戚和朋友在一起蓋房子，村落就形成了。

   c. There were water wells, street lights, streets and so on. 村裏有水井、路燈和街道等。

   d. The presence of a water well meant that people could drink hygienic and healthy water which would extend their lifespans. It also meant that the level of civilization of society developed. 水井意味著人們能喝到乾淨、健康的飲用水，能提高人們的壽命，也意味著社會的文明進步。

Project 研究項目

1. Business center. 貿易中心。
2. Main communication lines/military bases/pass/major mine areas. 主要交通樞紐、軍事基地、關口或礦區。
3. Government site, etc. 政府所在地等。

Exercise 3 P.17　練習 3　第 17 頁

1. 1）田　　2）土　　3）門　　4）馬　　5）牛　　6）爺　　7）羊　　8）豬

2. a. Horses can carry heavy goods. Cattle can help people plough their farmland. Sheep were good to eat. Pigs can be raised easily to support families (refer to the word formations). 養馬可以馱物，養牛可以犁地，養羊可以吃肉（根據繁體字「養」），養豬可以養家。

   b. A pig is a treasure to human beings. Its hair can be made into a brush. Its skin can be made into leather. Its white meat can be used as cooking oil and lamp oil. Its meat can be delicious. Its bone can be made into tools. Its pancreas can be made into soap. Its bladder can be made into a soccer ball. 豬對人來說渾身都是寶、牠的毛可以做刷子、牠的皮可以做皮革、牠的肥肉可以做炒菜用的油和燈油、牠的肉是美味的食品、牠的骨頭可以做成工具、牠的胰子可以做出肥皂、牠的膀胱可以做成足球。

   c. " 牛 (Cattle/oxen/cow)" can produce milk, beaf and leather. Their horns can be made into tools and carved into ornaments. Cattle also can work for human beings. 牛可以生產牛奶、牛肉和牛皮。牠的角可以做成工具和手工藝品，牛也可以為人類工作。

   d. Mother is pronounced like horse because it has the Sound Radical " 馬 ". The ancient Chinese thought mothers took care of their family like a busy horse (western people say "like a busy bee"). So we should show them our respect. 「媽」字的聲旁是馬，所

所以發音很像馬。古代中國人認為媽媽們也像馬一樣整天為全家奔忙（西方人認為忙得像蜜蜂），我們應該尊重她。

Project 研究項目

1. They hunted animals and picked fruits, nuts and plants. They also raised animals for meat and planted some crops and vegetables near where they lived. 他們打獵、採集野果、堅果和飼養小動物，將小植物或種子種在他們的住所附近。
2. They made clothes out of tree bark or leaves and animals' skin. 他們用樹皮、樹葉和動物的皮做衣服。
3. They lived in caves, under cliffs, on trees, tree hollows or put up huts with grass and tree branches. They could make simple tools from stones or bones and they used fire to cook their food. 他們住在山洞裏、山崖下、樹上或樹洞裏，或者用樹枝和草搭建草棚。他們能用石頭和骨頭做簡單的工具和用火做飯。

Exercise 4 P.23　練習4　第23頁

1. 1）孩　　2）男　　3）家　　4）奶　　5）婆　　6）公　　7）夫　　8）女
2. a. It reflects the traditional Chinese idea which is that the youngest son and the eldest grandson are the favourites of their seniors. 它反映中國傳統的思想，小兒子和大孫子是父母的寵兒。
   b. It means that the person has a very sad face. 它說明這個人有一張悲哀的臉。
   c. He should be a heroic man. He had to hunt and protect his family from wild animals and dangerous enemies. 他應該是像英雄一樣的人物。因為他要打獵和保護家人，避免野獸和危險的野蠻人。

Project 研究項目

1. Parents taught us the knowledge of life, such as how to take care of ourselves and avoid dangers. 父母教我們生活的知識，如何照顧我們自己和躲避危險。
2. Parents taught us how to do housework. 父母教我們怎樣做家務。
3. Parents taught us how to relate to other people, such as making friends and resolving conflicts. 父母教我們怎樣和其他人打交道，如交朋友和解決衝突。

Exercise 5 P.29　練習5　第29頁

1. 1）哥　　2）趙　　3）起　　4）走　　5）足　　6）己　　7）趕　　8）罪
2. a. The modern Chinese word for "foot" looks like a walking image, but the ancient one looks like a child observing his foot. It is used as a radical now. 現代漢字「足」很象走的樣子，而古代漢字「足」很像一個孩子在看自己的腳。古代的「足」做了現代漢語中的偏旁。
   b. Soccer originally came from China. 足球起源於中國。
   c. Xiao Zhao's work is to make the lazy men in the village work on the farm. He is a brave and responsible man. 小趙的工作是將村裏的懶漢趕到地裏幹活。他是勇敢和工作負責的人。
   d. Diligent. 勤勞。

Project 研究項目

1. Diligent. 勤勞。　2. Love their families. 熱愛家庭。　3. Love learning and saving money. 熱愛學習和節儉。

Exercise 6 P.35　練習6　第35頁

1. 1）姐　　2）妹　　3）姐　　4）第　　5）竹　　6）伯　　7）叔　　8）尖
2. a. Older children in Chinese traditional families were supposed to support their parents and help raise their siblings. 傳統的中國家庭大哥哥和大姐姐要幫助父母養育他們的弟弟、妹妹們。
   b. In China, the youngest and weakest were always considered first. 在中國，弱小的總是優先。
   c. According to Chinese traditional philosophy, a man has to earn money for his family, plant crops and do the farm work. Ladies had to raise children, do housework and take care of their seniors. 男人要掙錢養家、種莊稼和幹農活。女人要養孩子、做家務和照管老人。
   d. Elderly family members may help young parents with the care and education of the children. 老人們會幫助年輕的父母照顧和教育孩子。

Project 研究項目

Open answers. 開放式答案。

Exercise 7 P.41　練習7　第41頁

1. 1）哥　　2）嬸　　3）伯　　4）弟　　5）娘　　6）姨　　7）嫂　　8）妹
2. a. A mother's family lived far away from a father's family, because the word " 姨 aunt (mother's sister)" was formed by the Female Radical and "foreign tribe". There are two words " 外婆 (mother's mother)", the first word " 外 " means outside and the second word " 婆 " means an old lady, " 外婆 " can be explained that an old lady came from outside the tribe. This shows that since ancient times, Chinese people have known how to avoid non-blood-related marriage. 母親的娘家住在離父親家很遠的地方，因為「姨」字是由女字旁和東夷的「夷」（外族）組成的。「外婆」也是由外族的「外」和婆」組成的。說明中國人在遠古的時候就知道避免近親結婚的道理。

b. The eldest uncle, the second elder uncle and the youngest uncle. The first aunt, the second aunt and the youngest aunt. 大伯，二伯，小叔；大姑，二姑，小姑。

c. The eldest uncle, the second elder uncle and the youngest uncle, the first aunt, the second aunt and the youngest aunt. 大舅，二舅，小舅；大姨，二姨，小姨。

Project 研究項目

1. In China, " 紅娘 " is called a "go-between". Normally she is an old lady who introduces a young man and a young lady for the purpose of marriage. The young people may live far away from each other or from a village nearby. By using a go-between, The Chinese people have avoided blood-related marriages. 「紅娘」就是介紹人，往往是一個老婦人，她將遠方或鄰村的年輕男女介紹到一起結婚。這樣中國人就避免了近血緣的婚姻。

2. There are many reasons for a country coming into existence. The major ones are: 一個國家的形成有許多原因。主要的有：
   a. Political reasons. 政治原因。
   b. Economic reasons. 經濟原因。
   c. Religious reasons, etc. 宗教原因等。

Exercise 8 P.47   練習 8   第 47 頁

1. 1）夕   2）名   3）姓   4）瑰   5）竹   6）罪   7）鬼   8）晚

2. a   " 姓 " is formed by a female radical and the word " 生 (born/bear)", so we can guess that in ancient times, people use their mothers' surnames (the lady who gave birth to me). 「姓」是由一個女字旁和出生的「生」字組成的，因此我們可以猜測在古代，人們的姓是隨母親的 (姓：生我的女人）。

   b. The night is the time when people need a rest and a sleep. Parents scared their children into being quiet by saying that the night was haunted by the ghosts. They would take the child away if he shouted people's names or responded to other children's yelling. 夜間是人們休息和睡覺的時間。大人為了讓孩子安靜，就會嚇唬小孩說：夜晚是鬼出沒的時候，如果大聲喊別人的名字或者答應別人的喊叫，鬼就會把他抓走。

   c. It was said that the ghosts took people's souls away during the night. In order to get the right people, the ghosts shouted their names according to the lists given by the King of Hell. 據說鬼在夜間來取人的靈魂，為了找到這些人，鬼就會根據閻王給的名單喊他們的名字。

Project 研究項目

1. Open answers. 開放式答案。

2. In ancient China, they arrested criminals with the handcuffs which were made of wood. 在古代中國，罪犯是用木頭做的手銬逮捕。

Exercise 9 P.53   練習 9   第 53 頁

1. 1）夜   2）肉   3）魚   4）叫   5）年   6）客   7）春   8）天

2. a. They eat dumplings, sticky rice cakes, seafood and meat, etc. 他們吃餃子、年糕、海鮮和肉等。
   b. Relatives will visit each other on the first three days, then their friends and colleagues. 春節的前三天親戚互訪，然後是朋友和同事互相做客。
   c. They will carry wine, fruit and special products from their hometowns and also the gifts for children. 他們帶酒、水果、地方特產或孩子們的禮物。

3. Reading Comprehension. 閱讀理解
   1）元旦
   2）在趙小春的家
   3）姐姐
   4）十一口人
   5）Open answers. 開放式答案。

Project 研究項目

1. 三羊開泰（up），老人孩子年年好（left），哥姐弟妹節節安（right）。

2. Up: Eating fish is a Chinese traditional custom during Chinese New Year. " 水 (Water)", " 羊 (sheep)" and " 開 (open)" in spring indicate that it will be a prosperous year. 過年吃魚是中國人的一個傳統，春天有「水」、「羊」和「開」象徵著繁榮的一年。
   Left:The elderly and children will be healthy during the year. 左聯：老人和孩子每一年都健康。
   Right: Siblings will be safe when they travel on holidays. 右聯：兄弟姐妹每個節日出門旅遊都平平安安。

Vocabulary
詞彙

1.	人	human/man	41.	羊	sheep	81.	訟	litigate
2.	洞	cave	42.	豬	pig	82.	杖	cane
3.	同	together/with	43.	門	door	83.	仗	battle
4.	家	home/family	44.	闖	rush	84.	扶	support
5.	豚	pig/pork	45.	媽	mother	85.	伕	labour
6.	看	see/watch	46.	爸	father	86.	哥	elder brother
7.	好	good/well	47.	爺	grandfather	87.	走	walk
8.	子	son/child	48.	略	strategy	88.	足	foot
9.	女	female/woman	49.	苗	seedling	89.	趙	a surname
10.	會	can	50.	去	go	90.	赳	valiantly
11.	你	you	51.	城	city	91.	趟	measure word
12.	婦	woman	52.	馱	carry	92.	趕	drive
13.	安	safe	53.	駒	foal	93.	起	get up
14.	孫	grandson	54.	美	beauty	94.	己	self
15.	學	learn	55.	羔	lamb	95.	罪	crime
16.	銅	copper	56.	問	ask	96.	罷	strike
17.	筒	tube	57.	閃	sparkle	97.	路	road
18.	嫁	marry (for woman)	58.	螞	ant	98.	跑	run
19.	稼	crop	59.	罵	curse	99.	歌	song
20.	字	word	60.	洋	ocean	100.	糾	correct
21.	籽	seed	61.	鮮	fresh	101.	淌	drip
22.	取	get/take	62.	悶	boring	102.	躺	lie down
23.	娶	marry (for man)	63.	們	plural	103.	桿	pole
24.	房	house	64.	力	labour/power	104.	肝	liver
25.	戶	household	65.	男	male/man	105.	記	memorise
26.	村	village	66.	老	old/senior	106.	紀	discipline
27.	落	fall/to place	67.	孩	children	107.	姐	elder sister
28.	街	street	68.	奶	grandmother	108.	且	even/just
29.	井	well	69.	妻	wife	109.	妹	younger sister
30.	螢	firefly	70.	婆	old lady	110.	未	not yet
31.	松	pine tree	71.	公	old man	111.	弟	younger brother
32.	行	walking	72.	兒	son	112.	第	a function word
33.	方	square	73.	子	son/child	113.	竹	bamboo
34.	放	set free	74.	丈	1/3rd meter	114.	伯	elder uncle
35.	按	press	75.	夫	husband	115.	白	white
36.	案	case	76.	助	assist/help	116.	叔	younger uncle
37.	田	farmland	77.	孝	obedience	117.	尖	pinpoint
38.	土	soil/land	78.	谷	valley	118.	笑	laugh
39.	馬	horse	79.	該	should	119.	這	this
40.	牛	cattle	80.	松	a pine tree	120.	送	send

121.	睨	look sideways		160.	牲	animal
122.	泊	park		161.	餓	hungry
123.	淚	fail		162.	年	year
124.	菽	beans		163.	節	festival
125.	姨	aunt (mother's sisters)		164.	春	spring
126.	夷	foreign (ancient)		165.	天	day/the sky
127.	娘	girl/mum		166.	開	open
128.	良	kind		167.	夜	night
129.	臼	mortar/joint		168.	客	guest
130.	舅	uncle (mother's brothers)		169.	各	individual
131.	姑	aunt (father's sisters)		170.	笑	laugh
132.	古	ancient		171.	叫	bark/cry/call
133.	嫂	sister-in-law (elder brother's wife)		172.	格	square
134.	叟	a sound radical		173.	閣	cabinet
135.	嬸	aunt-in-law (younger uncle's wife)		174.	漁	fishing
				175.	毒	poison
136.	審	examine		176.	泰	prosperous
137.	稂	grain				
138.	踉	stumble				
139.	故	former/story				
140.	搜	search				
141.	艘	a measure word				
142.	瀋	a place name				
143.	表	watch/cousin				
144.	堂	hall/cousin				
145.	您	you (respect)				
146.	姓	surname				
147.	生	bear/produce				
148.	夕	sunset				
149.	名	name				
150.	鬼	ghost				
151.	晚	late/evening				
152.	瑰	rose				
153.	槐	pagoda tree				
154.	黨	party (politics)				
155.	夢	dream				
156.	馳	gallop				
157.	池	pool				
158.	性	gender				
159.	星	star				